Guilty?

by

Eric Brown

Illustrated by Alan Marks

First published in 2009 in Great Britain by
Barrington Stoke Ltd
18 Walker St, Edinburgh, EH3 7LP

www.barringtonstoke.co.uk

ISBN: 978-1-84299-688-1

Printed in Great Britain by Bell & Bain Ltd

A Note from the Author

I wanted to write a story about a boy who was being bullied, and what he did about it. I also wanted to write a story about knife crime. I wanted to show how awful it was to be bullied – but also how awful it might be if you decided to do something about it ... These days, more and more people are carrying knives – and more people are using them.

I wanted to ask the question: what would you do if you were being bullied every week, and the bully was taking money from you? How angry would you get? How far would you go to stop someone from bullying you?

In the story, Nicky attacks the bully.

Nicky says he only beat up the bully, but now the bully is dead.

Did Nicky kill him?

What do you think?

To Alex, Robyn,
Maddie, Emilie & Freya

Contents

Chapter 1

Kev

I was walking home from school. It was another Friday.

On Fridays, most kids think about the weekend and what they are going to do on Saturday and Sunday. Play football. Watch TV. Go to the cinema. Meet friends.

But for me, Nicky Green, Fridays are the worst day of the week. Every Friday I meet Kev Carson in Town Park. He's always waiting for me, with his hands deep in his pockets and his big ugly head tucked away under his hood.

It's always the same. He always smiles at me as if I'm his best mate. Then he asks me for a fiver. I give him the cash, and he still beats me up.

He said that if I didn't give him the cash, then he'd kill me.

That's how it is most Fridays. But today will be different. Today will be very different.

Chapter 2

Attack

I came to the trees where I meet Kev.
I felt sick.

He smiled. But it wasn't a real smile. It
was a horrible grin. He had one tooth
missing, and a tattoo on his neck – a grinning
skull.

I looked round me. There was no one else in the park. We were all alone.

"Hiya, Nicky," he said. "How's things? Got my fiver?"

"What do you think?" I said, in a soft voice.

"I hope you've got me my fiver. 'Cos if you don't have it, I'll break your sodding legs. Then I'll kick your face in."

I stared at him. He was loving this. He was grinning like the skull tattoo on his neck.

"So ..." He held out his hand. "A fiver. In my hand, Nicky boy."

My heart was beating so fast I felt it was going to explode. I stared at him and said, "Sod off."

His face froze. He didn't think I would say that. No one had ever told bully-boy Kev to sod off before.

He said, very slowly, "What did you say, Nicky boy?"

"I said, 'sod off'. You're not getting a fiver, now or ever again."

He grinned. "Oh, I like that! Nicky boy, acting big! Well, I want my fiver or I'll –"

And that's when I jumped on him.

Chapter 3

Anger

I had a lot of anger inside me. I had weeks and weeks of anger, just waiting to explode.

I hit him in the face, and he punched me in the belly. I dived at him and knocked him to the ground. He didn't think I could get

that angry. We rolled over and over, hitting each other.

Then I was on top of him, and I punched his face again and again. He pushed me off him, and I jumped to my feet. He stood up, staring at me. He looked like an angry bull, about to charge.

He ran at me ...

Chapter 4

Blood

Moments later Kev Carson was lying on the ground and I was staring at him. There was a lot of blood on his hoodie. I looked at my hands and my white school shirt. They had blood all over them.

I looked around. The park was still empty.

First, I had to clean away the blood before I went home. I ran past the trees to the toilet block. Inside I washed my hands and tried to get the blood out of my shirt. A lot came off, but my shirt still looked pink.

I looked up, into the mirror. I was grinning. I was grinning like a fool – and do you know something?

I felt great. For the first time in months, I felt fantastic.

I mean – what would you have felt like?

I left the park and ran off home. My heart was still beating fast. I thought of Kev Carson, lying in the park in a pool of blood. *Well*, I thought, *he won't be bullying me again.*

I was thinking about Kev when I bumped into a guy.

I was walking around the corner, with my head down. I wasn't looking where I was going, and I just banged into this guy a bit older than me.

"Hey!" he yelled. "Watch where you're going, you little git!"

Then he looked down at the ground. A knife was lying by his feet. It was wet with blood. He looked hard at it, then pushed past

me and rushed away down the street. I looked around. No one had seen us.

I bent down at once and picked up the knife. Stupid, I know, but I just didn't think. I slipped it into my pocket and ran home.

Chapter 5

Knife

I hid the knife under my bed. I pulled off my shirt and stuffed it behind the bookcase. I got a clean shirt from the shelf.

I pulled the fiver from the pocket of my jeans and smiled to myself. I could see Kev,

lying in the park in a pool of blood – and I didn't feel sorry for him at all.

That night I had dinner with Mum and Dad in the kitchen. The TV was on, and Dad was moaning about the state of the world as he always does.

"You're looking pleased with yourself," Mum said to me.

I nodded. "Scored three goals today," I lied.

"Three goals," Dad said. "Hat-trick hero. We'll have you playing for the Arsenal yet."

The local news was on the TV.

A reporter was standing by some trees. I stared at the screen. My heart was pounding again.

The reporter said, "... Kevin Carson was 15, and a pupil at Grove School. His body was found in the park behind me at around 5pm today ..."

I left the rest of my dinner and went up to my room. I lay on the bed and stared at the wall.

Kev Carson was dead. Never again would he bully me – or anyone else.

What did I feel?

What would you feel?

Chapter 6

Dreams

Later that night, when it was dark, I remembered the knife under the bed. And I thought about the blood on my shirt.

What if Mum found the knife and the shirt when she was doing my room? Would

she think about the stabbing in the park?
Would she think that I'd done it?

I had a long think about what I should do.
Then I had an idea.

At midnight, I got dressed and got the
knife from under the bed. I pulled my shirt
from behind the bookcase and put the knife
and the shirt into a brown paper bag. I
opened my bedroom door. The house was
silent. Mum and Dad were in bed. I crept
down the stairs. I took the key from its hook
in the hall, and let myself out of the house.

It was a warm night. I ran through the empty streets. When I got to the trees in the park, I was going to chuck the bag into the pond. But the bag would float. That would be a big mistake.

So I hid the bag under some bushes. No one would ever find it there. I put lots of twigs and leaves over it, then I went home.

I let myself into the house, crept up the stairs and went to bed.

I lay in the dark, thinking about Kev Carson. He was dead. He would never bully anyone again. He'd never play football again, or watch his favourite team, Man United.

I slept, and had dreams about Kev Carson. He was chasing me, and he had blood all over him.

I woke up suddenly. I cried out and sat up. I was damp with sweat and panting hard.

Then I finally understood that I had been a fool. What if the cops found the bag? They would inspect the knife and find my finger-prints on it. And they would get my DNA from the shirt I had been wearing.

I had to go and get the bag back before the cops found it.

I looked at the clock. It was 7.30am. A minute later Mum called up the stairs, "Nicky. Get up. Time for school!"

I had a quick breakfast and ran out of the house.

I would go to the park, find the brown paper bag and hide it in my school bag.

I walked into the park and ran to where I'd hidden the paper bag.

Then I stopped and stared.

Three coppers were standing by the bushes. There was black and yellow tape shutting off that whole bit of the wood. Cops with sniffer dogs were everywhere, hunting in the bushes.

I set off for school. But I felt sick.

Chapter 7

Bully

Everyone was talking about Kev Carson that morning.

"Have you heard?" a girl said. "He was stabbed to death in the park last night. Ten times, the news said. The knife went right into his heart."

A lad said, "I liked Kev. He was a good mate. Me and him, we went to watch Man United at Chelsea last season."

"Yeah," someone else said. "He was a good mate, Kev was."

Another boy said, "But he was a bully. He beat up kids smaller than him. Some people deserve to die."

A girl looked hard at the boy. "That's horrible! You can't say that!"

The lad said, "But he *was* a bully. A thug. He beat up kids just for fun."

"He may have been a bully now," the girl said, "but he could have grown up to be sorry about what he did to those kids. He could have grown up to do something good with his life. Now he hasn't got that chance ..."

The girl looked at me. "What do you think, Nicky?"

I just shook my head.

Kev Carson was a bully. He made my life hell. But did he deserve to die?

What did I think?

Chapter 8

Sick

All morning I was thinking about the knife and my shirt with the blood on it. What if the cops found them in the brown paper bag? What would they do then? What would I say?

I felt sick.

I was in Maths when Mrs Brown from the school office knocked on the door and came into the room. She said something to the teacher so softly we couldn't hear what it was.

The teacher looked across the room at me. My heart started to bang against my ribs. My face went red.

"Nicky Green," the teacher said. "The head-teacher would like to see you in her office. Off you go."

Everyone stared at me as I got up and left the classroom with Mrs Brown. I could feel the blood throbbing in my ears. I was hot and I felt dizzy.

Two cops were speaking to the head-teacher in her office. They looked at me when I walked into the room.

"Nicky Green?" said the tall one. "We would like to take you down to the police station, where we will ask you about what you were doing last night ..."

He put a hand on my arm and led me from the school.

Chapter 9

Murder

They drove me to the police station and took me into a room like an office. My dad was there. He was sitting on a chair by the door. He just looked at me. He didn't say a word.

I looked away. I couldn't look at him.
I felt even more awful with my dad there.

The cops took my finger-prints, and then
a cutting from my hair – a DNA sample, they
said.

The cops took me to an interview room
and locked me in. I was there for about two
hours, and then the door opened. The same
two cops came in, and then my dad.

The tall cop held up two plastic bags.

I was shaking with fear.

"Right, Nicky Green," the tall cop said. "You're here on the 14th of July, 2009, with Detective Inspector James, that's me, and PC Brook. Also with us is George Green, the father of you, the suspect ..." He went on like this for a time.

Then the other cop said, "You are here so we can ask you some questions about the murder of Kevin Carson, which took place in Town Park at about 5pm yesterday afternoon, 13th of July, 2009."

I shook my head. "I don't know anything about it," I said. I wanted to say it in a loud voice, but I was so afraid that it came out as a croak.

"Oh, no?" said Detective Inspector James. "Well, we'll see about that." And he lifted the plastic bags onto the table and said, "Have you seen these before?"

I stared at the bags. Inside the first one was my shirt covered in blood. In the other was the knife.

I shook my head. "Never seen them before in my life," I said.

My father moved. He was holding his head in his hands. I think he was crying to himself.

Detective Inspector James smiled. "You haven't? Then how come your finger-prints are all over the knife?"

I stared at the two cops. I felt dizzy. I was going to be sick.

They were going to charge me with murder. I'd spend the rest of my life in prison.

Chapter 10

Did I Do It?

"We want the truth!" Detective Inspector James said.

PC Brook said, "You met Kevin Carson in the park last night. You had a fight with him. During the fight, you pulled a knife and stabbed Carson to death."

Dad turned and looked at me. "Tell them the truth, Nicky. Tell *me* the truth – did you do it?"

I shook my head. "No, it's not true. I didn't do it!"

The cop went on, "Then you put the shirt and the knife in a bag and hid it in the bushes in the park. It will be better for you if you own up. That's what you did, isn't it?"

My mouth was dry. I said, "No, it wasn't like that."

"Then what did you do?" Detective Inspector James asked.

I licked my lips. "I did meet Kev in the park, that's true. And we did fight. He was a bully, see? He wanted a fiver from me. We had a fight, and that's how I got blood on my shirt."

PC Brook was smiling. "And the knife? Just how did you get your finger-prints on the knife?"

I nodded. "You see, later, after I left the park … I was walking down the street. I wasn't looking where I was going, and I bumped into this guy. And … and he must have dropped the knife. I mean, he looked scared, and he was panting hard as if he was running away from something …"

The cops looked at me. I could see that they didn't believe a word I was saying. I was wet with sweat. I looked at my dad. He was wiping tears from his eyes.

I went on, "Anyway, this guy ran off without picking the knife up."

"So what did you do then?" PC Brook asked.

"I picked up the knife. I mean, it looked like a good one."

"And you didn't see that there was blood on it?" Detective Inspector James said.

I shook my head. "No," I said.

The men were silent. There wasn't a sound in the room and I could hear my heart beating. It was thumping in my ears.

PC Brook rubbed his eyes as if he was very tired. "Look, Nicky, we know you stabbed Carson to death."

"No, I didn't!" I yelled.

He went on, "We know you had a reason to kill him. This story about bumping into a guy who dropped a knife ... it's just that,

Nicky, a story. Admit it. We know you killed Kevin Carson. We know you did it."

I stared at the cops. I felt ill. I wanted to run away. I knew that all the facts pointed at me ...

I looked at my dad, and shook my head.

"We know you killed him!" said Detective Inspector James.

"But I didn't," I said softly.

****

And that's my story.

Did the bully, Kevin Carson, deserve to die?

Have I told you the truth? Or have I lied to you?

Did I kill him? Or was he killed by the guy who I bumped into in the street?

Will I be sent to prison for the murder of Kev Carson?

Well, *what do you think?*

Barrington Stoke would like to thank all its readers for commenting on the manuscript before publication and in particular:

Christopher Dolan
Michael Hamilton
Thomas Jones
Robbie Madden
Leanna McCarthy
Andrew Murphy
Nathan Murphy
Ian Petrie
Nathan Stevenson
Colleen Stowe
Richard Warwicker

Become a Consultant!

Would you like to give us feedback on our titles before they are published? Contact us at the email address below – we'd love to hear from you!

info@barringtonstoke.co.uk
www.barringtonstoke.co.uk

Great reads – no problem!

Barrington Stoke books are:

Great stories – from thrillers to comedy to horror, and all by the best writers around!

No hassle – fast reads with no boring bits, and a story that doesn't let go of you till the last page.

Short – the perfect size for a fast, fun read.

We use our own font and paper to make it easier to read our books. And we ask teenagers like you, who want a no-hassle read, to check every book before it's published.

That way, we know for sure that every Barrington Stoke book is a great read for everyone.

Check out www.barringtonstoke.co.uk for more info about Barrington Stoke and our books!

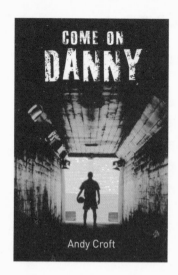

**Come On, Danny
by
Andy Croft**

Danny's dad is in prison.
His teachers are on his case.
His friends are on his back.
Can he find a way out?

**Two Words
by
Tanya Landman**

Two friends.
A hiking trip.
A mistake that changes everything.

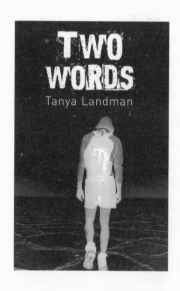

You can order these books directly from our website at
www.barringtonstoke.co.uk

Don't Call Us
by
Pat Thomson

The gang want Jack to help them steal some games consoles.
They will get him if he says no.
What can he do?

Mind-Set
by
Joanna Kenrick

Mark and Shaleem are best mates.
But the bombs change everything.
Will Mark stand up for Shaleem when it matters?

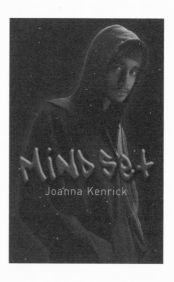

You can order these books directly from our website at
www.barringtonstoke.co.uk